Up to Low

ALSO BY BRIAN DOYLE

Up to Low

Brian Doyle

A Groundwood Book
Douglas & McIntyre
Toronto Vancouver Buffalo

Groundwood Books/Douglas & McIntyre
585 Bloor Street West
Toronto, Ontario M6G 1K5

Distributed in the U.S. by Publishers Group West
4065 Hollis Street
Emeryville, CA 94608

The publisher gratefully acknowledges the assistance of the
Canada Council and the Ontario Arts Council.

Library of Congress Data is available

Canadian Cataloguing in Publication Data

Doyle, Brian
Up to low

ISBN 0-88899-264-5

I. Title.

PS8557.087U6 1996   jC813'.54   C95-933039-9
PZ7.D68Up 1996

Cover illustration by Ludmilla Temertey
Printed and bound in Canada

Thanks to my wife Jackie, the classiest of ladies, who teaches that to leave something of you behind is your reason on earth.

UP TO LOW

PART
I

We hadn't been up to Low since my mother died two years before. Aunt Dottie was living with us now so Dad and I were going to go up ahead to clean the cabin up and then she was going to come up later. You see, Aunt Dottie was very clean and Dad knew that she would be unhappy if there was dirt around or any germs or crud in the cabin.

Aunt Dottie always covered her face when she coughed and when anyone else coughed too. And she always wiped her feet three times each on the mat, and not on the same place on the mat either. And she never used anyone else's spoon or took a bite of anyone else's apple and she didn't like me to do these things either. And always put toilet paper on the seat if you're at somebody else's house. And never touch the toothpaste tube on your toothbrush when you're putting on toothpaste. And always rub the cucumber ends against the cucumber to get the poison out. And don't eat candy unless it's wrapped. And always wipe yourself three times.

And all that.

We were packing and Aunt Dottie was helping us. Dad was talking about Mean Hughie, one of his old rivals.

"They tell me Mean Hughie's going to die," he was saying as he rolled up a pair of pants and shoved them into his suitcase.

"And don't drink the water unless you boil it first," Aunt Dottie was saying as she took out the rolled up pants, folded them, wrapped them in sheets of tissue paper and put them carefully back in the suitcase.

"Yes," Dad was saying, "Mean Hughie's got the cancer, they tell me. I'll believe it when I see it. I think he's too mean to die." He was firing socks into a knapsack.

"And after you kill flies," Aunt Dottie was saying, "be sure you wrap them each in little tissues and burn them." She was taking the socks from the knapsack and spraying each of them with Lysol and placing them in little individual bags. "And the same if you blow your nose," she said. "Blow it in a little tissue and burn it right away."

"Mean Hughie is the meanest man in the Gatineau," Dad was saying, while Aunt Dottie was in the kitchen scrubbing the bottoms of our shoes with steel wool and Dutch Cleanser.

"And don't step in anything around that farm," she called over the sound of the taps running.

"Yesser," Dad was saying, "if Mean Hughie dies, he'll have to go somewhere, but I can't for the life of me guess where it is they'd send him. Heaven's out of the question and Hell's too nice a spot for him."

12

"And be sure when you pick berries to wash them in this Lysol before you eat them," Aunt Dottie said as she placed a large jar of Lysol in the big knapsack.

It was finally time to go.

We said good-bye to Aunt Dottie, and when I went to kiss her she turned her face away and I got her on the ear.

Germs, I guess.

She promised she'd see us in a couple of weeks.

"It'll take her a month to get ready," Dad was saying as we went down the stairs. "It'll be a month before she's clean enough to even leave the house!"

We had two army backpacks that Dad had brought back from the war and two old suitcases. We walked down to St. Patrick Street to wait for the streetcar.

There are two kinds of streetcars: tall and short. My favourite are the tall ones. They seem to me to be more intelligent looking. They have a serious look on their faces. And they rock side to side in an easy kind of way. A way that makes everybody lean together. The person you sit beside can lean on you a bit and you can hold a bit stiff until it is time to lean the other way and then he can do the same. This way you are always touching, back and forward, as though you are one person. It is very friendly. The short streetcars are different. They snap and whip and make people sitting together bump each other and crash around in the seat so that you can't think straight.

The streetcar we got on was a tall one and Dad and I put our back packs and suitcases on one seat and sat in another. We were rocking from side to side down St. Patrick Street, nice and even and easy, and I was thinking about Mean Hughie.

Mean Hughie and his big, poor family and the farmhouse they lived in with the daylight coming through between the logs and the crooked floor and the broken furniture. I had only been there once, when I was a kid. My mother sent me over to buy some raisin bread from Mean Hughie's wife, Poor Bridget. That was her name. Poor Bridget. Everybody called her that because of what she had to put up with. Poor Bridget was standing at her kitchen table, up to her elbows in flour, punching a big lump of bread dough and sprinkling raisins on it while about a million flies buzzed around competing with the raisins. And everywhere you'd look there was a kid peeking, very shy, from behind something or from under something. Kids under Poor Bridget's dress, behind chairs, under the table, behind the stove, peeking out the cellar door, behind the butter churn, and from under an old bed in the corner where their grandfather was lying like a corpse with his mouth open.

The bread that was already baked was stacked, hot, at the end of the table. Poor Bridget swept the flies off the stack with her hand and gave me three loaves. They were too hot to hold, and since she had no paper or bags or anything I took off my shirt and wrapped the bread in it.

Just as I was handing her the fifty cents for the bread I felt the room get dark. It was Mean Hughie at the open door behind me. He filled the whole doorway blocking out most of the light. I could hear him breathing. Suddenly every kid's face disappeared. Like a dozen groundhogs ducking down in an open field.

"I'll take that fifty cents. That way it'll be nice and safe!" says Mean Hughie.

I dropped the five dimes in his big lumpy hand while Mean Hughie nailed me with his eyes and let a big slow grin open up the bottom of his face.

"How's your father!"

"Fine thank you, sir," I said, extra polite.

"Good," says Mean Hughie. "Let's hope he stays that way!"

I tied the sleeves of my shirt in a knot and slung the bread over my shoulder. On my way out of the yard I heard Mean Hughie growl something and I heard a slap.

As I turned the corner around the barn I almost

bumped into the oldest of the kids. She was about my age and she was carrying a tin pan of chicken feed in her right hand. Her left arm was missing from the elbow down. Her dress was raggedy and her feet were bare. We stood there staring at each other until I heard her mother call from the house. There was a sad sort of crack in her voice.

"Baby Bridget, Baby Bridget," she called.

Baby Bridget looked quickly at the house, back at me, and then stepped around me without saying a word.

Sitting there on the streetcar, swaying from side to side against my dad, I was seeing the whole thing again. And especially one thing above all else. More than the hot bread against my back and the sound of the slap and the flies and raisins and all the dirty-faced little kids and Mean Hughie's ugly grin. More than all that. More than all that was the colour and the shape of Baby Bridget's eyes. They were eyes that were deep green. The deep green of the Gatineau hills. The eyes that took me in and made my tongue thick so I couldn't speak. The greenest green. And their shape was the shape of the petals of the trillium.

Right on the corner of Dalhousie and St. Patrick the trolley pole came off the wire and the streetcar went dead. I was beside the open window so I had a good look as the driver walked along outside the car to put the pole back on. He was taking his time and he had a nice look on his face. Everything else was stopped. All the pedestrians with their parcels or their push carts or their canes stopped to watch. All the cars were stopped and the people were leaning out the windows to watch. A streetcar behind us and one coming on the opposite track were stopped and all the people were hanging out the windows to watch. The storekeepers along both sides of St. Patrick and Dalhousie came to their doors or stood in their windows. Upstairs the people in the apartments over the shops, older people, in dressing gowns and underwear tops, leaned on their windowsills and watched.

Everybody was taking a break. Taking a break on a nice day in late June at the corner of St. Patrick and Dalhousie about one o'clock in the afternoon. They all wanted to watch the sparks when the driver put the pole back on the wire.

When the pole sparked, the generators came back on, and everybody gave the driver a little bit of applause and some car horns.

Before we got off at York and Dalhousie, Dad slipped the bottle of Lysol out of the big knapsack and left it under the seat.

"Ruins the taste of the berries," he said and, gave me a big wink.

There were some things you just didn't let on to Aunt Dottie. Like leaving the Lysol on the streetcar. There would be no use trying to tell her that we didn't want to lug a big jar of disinfectant around just because she thought all berries were infested with germs. It was easier just to leave it on the streetcar.

And another thing we didn't mention to Aunt Dottie was that we were taking Dad's friend Frank with us.

She'd have a fit if she knew that Frank was going to be there. She couldn't stand Frank. One of the reasons she couldn't stand him was that he used to pick his nose a bit when he was over at our place for supper. Not much. Just a bit. Most people wouldn't notice. But you'd have to be some great magician like Houdini or somebody to get away with picking your nose when Aunt Dottie was around. And he also put his beer bottle on her white doilies on the arm of the chesterfield.

And he didn't flush the toilet.

And last Christmas he fell head first into our Christmas tree and broke everything and nearly electrocuted himself on the lights.

So we didn't tell Aunt Dottie that Frank was coming. Dad said that by the time she got there, he'd be gone, anyway.

"The train leaves at two, so we'll have time to

go to the liquor store, get Frank out of the hotel, pick up some meat at the market, and be on our way," Dad was saying.

We went into the liquor store.

"Haven't seen Frank in a couple of weeks. Wonder what he's been up to," said Dad.

"Is he going to stay with us the whole time?" I asked.

"He's going to pitch a tent at the top of the hill behind the cabin. He'll be with us but he won't be with us if you know what I mean."

I knew what Dad meant. Frank was a nice guy, but sometimes his boozing would get you down.

Dad bought a bottle of gin and we headed down to York Street and into the Dominion Hotel where we were supposed to meet Frank.

I waited in a little back room and had a coke while Dad sat out with the men to wait for Frank. I was only half way through the coke when Dad came in and said the waiters told him that Frank was meeting us at the Union Station.

"It must be something horrible important to drag him out of this place," Dad said and we strapped on our packs and headed across to Aubrey's Meat Market.

We were standing in the sawdust on Hector Aubrey's floor and there was old Hector. He looked like a side of beef dressed in a white apron. He was chopping something very close to his thumb with a big flashing cleaver.

Dad was getting a ten pound chunk of corned beef and some other stuff from one of the other butchers, and old Hector, who knew everybody, spilled the news about Frank.

"I hear Frank bought a car," he said, as he wiped blood from his hands onto his huge apron. "Who's he goin' to get to drive it for him? You gonna be his driver, Tommy?" He was talking to Dad.

Everybody in the shop knew what he was talking about. Frank would be too drunk most of the time to drive a car, and the butchers and the customers were all talking and laughing about it. As we were leaving, old Hector said: "You could always get Young Tommy here to run ahead of the car and warn the innocent people along the Gatineau highway what it is that's in store for them!"

Everybody laughed at that too, and then we left.

Just as we got to the pillars of the Union Station a new car came staggering around the War Memorial, cut right across Confederation Square, rode up on the sidewalk in front of the station, and crunched into a lamp post right in front of us. Behind the wheel was Frank.

"It's true," said Dad under his breath, "he *did* buy a car."

It was a brand new 1950 Buick Special with Dynaflow transmission, eight cylinder engine, vertical grille bars and bomb-shaped parking lights mounted on the front bumper. It had three air vents on each side of the hood, whitewall tires and an aerial in the middle of the windshield pointing back with the wind, four door, wraparound bumpers, and teeth—nine big long teeth, chrome teeth, for a grille!

We threw our stuff in the back and Dad shoved Frank over into the passenger seat and backed the car off the post. We left two of Frank's new chrome teeth on the road beside the post. We eased nice and easy out into the traffic, turned on Sussex Street and headed over the Interprovincial Bridge.

"Frank, why didn't you tell us you bought a car?" Dad said, after he got used to the feel of her.

"I wanted to surprise you," Frank said. "It'll be faster than the train. And we can go anywhere we want once we get there."

"Surprise us! You pretty near ran us down!"

"She got away on me," said Frank. Then he let out a long beer burp.

It was a good thing Aunt Dottie wasn't there.

Away down below us, on the water, the huge log booms sat like pancakes.

A couple of tugs were churning away, looking like they'd never get anywhere. If you look at a tug hauling logs, then look away for a while, then look back, you can see that it's moved a bit. But if you just stare right at it, you'd think it wasn't moving at all.

"They tell me Mean Hughie's going to die," Dad was saying. "He's supposed to have the cancer."

"Believe it when I see it," said Frank. Then he went into a coughing fit.

The loose boards on the Interprovincial Bridge were slapping on the steel under our wheels and the black girders with the rivets were zipping by.

Frank coughed all the way over the bridge and most of the way through Hull until we stopped at Romanuk's for groceries.

They sold everything in Romanuk's: naptha for the Coleman lamp, minnows for bait, vegetables, beer, rubber boots, overalls, tools, candy, hats, egg lifters, bottle openers, spinners, canned potatoes, rosaries, lamps shaped like naked women, joke books, yoyos, seeds, shotgun shells, blood pudding, pork hocks, head cheese.

There was a deer head on the wall with a beer bottle stuck upside down on one of the points of his rack.

Mr. Romanuk gave Dad and Frank a shot of whisky

from underneath the counter while they talked about Mean Hughie.

I had two more cokes.

"Is dat the guy you hit with the shovel years ago, Tommy?"

"That's the lad, all right," said Dad. "Hit him a two-hander right over the forehead with a long-handled gravel shovel and they say he didn't even blink. Snapped his braces clean off. Got a head like a rock!"

I had heard the story many times before. I could picture it as though I'd been there, even though it happened before I was born.

Mean Hughie blinked all right, but he only blinked once, and then his eyes got narrower and narrower and he got staring out over the river and up to where the mountain meets the sky. Then he turned around and set out for home. I could see his big back and the blue shirt marked with the X where his braces were before Dad's blast with the shovel snapped them.

Dad was still talking. Dad loved to talk.

"He had a notion he was goin' to set fire to my cabin. I tried to explain to him, when I caught him, that he'd better not do that. Had to slap him with the shovel to get his attention. It cured him of that notion, anyway. I told him that if I ever came up the Gatineau and found my cabin burned, I wouldn't even ask any questions, I'd just take a gun and go over to his place . . ."

While Dad was talking I was thinking about Baby Bridget. When we got up to Low I was going to go over to her place again for some bread. I wondered what she'd be like. Three years. I wondered if her eyes were the same.

We got back in Frank's new car with the two missing teeth. Frank was driving again.

"Go nice and slow, Frank," Dad said and we took off up the road. Frank had one eye closed and he was aiming the car along our side of the road. There were black tracks where the tires made marks in the tar. Frank was trying to follow these tracks. There was no traffic for a while and Frank had the road to himself.

Dad was humming and singing his favourite song:

"The place where me heart was

You could easy roll a turnip in . . ."

It was a song about an Irish guy who lost his heart.

Up ahead, a truck pulled onto the road and headed our way.

"Can you get by this truck, Frank?"

Frank was hugging the right. The closer the truck got the more Frank hugged the right. Soon our right wheels were on the mud shoulder. He was giving the truck a lot of room. He had one eye closed and he was looking through the steering wheel. I guess he thought that if he closed one eye he could aim the car better. He looked like a guy trying to fire a rifle for the first time.

Frank was the worst driver on the whole Gatineau.

The truck was so close now that I could see the driver. He was looking at Frank like you would look at a rare, tropical, one-eyed fish in an aquarium. Our car was down to about ten miles an hour. Then all our wheels were in the soft grass and mud and we stopped very quietly against a pretty big rock. I heard another one of the Buick's teeth go.

We were leaning away over to our right so we had to get out Frank's side. That was hard because Frank had to get out first. And Frank was just sitting there and still steering.

The truck turned around and parked in front of us.

"Hello Frank!" said the driver as he opened our door and helped Frank out. "See you got a new car!"

"Good day, Baz" said Dad. "Got a chain in your truck?" Baz got out the chain and hooked us up.

"Heading up to Low?" said Baz. "Guess it's a lot handier with the car, eh Frank? No more waitin' on the train?"

"Yep," said Frank, "go anywhere we want to; freer'n birds." Then Frank played a little patt-i-cake with both hands on his pot. He always did this when he felt sort of proud of himself. Pitti-pat, pitti-pat, with the fingers of both hands, on his pot.

As Baz pulled Frank's new Buick out of the ditch, I could hear the train whistling down in the gully along the bank of the Gatineau. It was half-past-two.

We would've been on that train if Frank hadn't bought that car.

"I hear Mean Hughie's got the cancer and he's threatening to die," Baz was saying as we helped Frank to get back behind the wheel and Baz gave him a little drink of gin.

"I'll believe it when I see it," said Dad and we pulled away.

About a mile up the road we wheeled into the Avalon Hotel. Frank crunched his left fender a bit against the corner of the hotel as he tried to park.

I didn't hear any of the Buick's teeth fall this time.

It was going to take a long time to go the forty miles up to Low the way we were going.

Inside the Avalon it was damp and dark. The ceiling was low, and Dad had to duck his head a bit walking around in there. We sat at a table with some guys that Frank and Dad knew. Everybody had a quart of beer. I had another coke.

They were talking about Mean Hughie.

"Is it true he has the cancer and isn't long for this world?" said a guy with a big wart on his nose.

"That's what they say," another guy said. He had a great big face, red as blood. "But I'll believe it when I see it."

"He could never twist you Tommy, could he? I heard he twisted you, but I never believed it. I'd bet real money he never twisted you." It was the guy with the wart talking, who had wrists and arms almost as big as Dad's.

"He's put both my arms down at one time or another. But not in one sitting. Don't forget we been going at it since we worked breakin' rocks at the dam when we were only about fifteen years of age. So we've twisted many times. As of now I'd say we're about even. We were only about the age of Young Tommy here when we got started. We been feudin' since first we ever run into each other. I think it was because I was so handsome and good looking and he was so ugly and horrible looking . . ."

Dad, when he got started, was a pretty good talker. Most guys, when they talk, can only say a little bit and then they have to take a rest. But Dad, he could say a lot and pretty well keep everybody's attention.

He was talking about Mean Hughie and how every time anything bad or stupid happened to him he seemed to get uglier and meaner.

You could tell that Dad felt a little sorry for Mean Hughie because when he told about the worst thing that ever happened to him, he got quite serious and stopped making fun of him.

The worst thing that ever happened to Mean Hughie was there was an accident with his binder and his oldest kid had half her arm cut off. She was their first baby; Bridget her name was. Baby Bridget.

When we got back in the car I asked Dad what happened.

"They say the binder was stuck on a rock and Mean Hughie got off the binder to beat the horses and they reared up and ran a few steps and the little girl was in front of the knives to pick up a flower—clover, I guess. And the knives took her arm. It was a sad day for Mean Hughie. And they say he hit her for being in the way. It was a mean thing to do. And a sad day for both of them."

Frank was trying to back the car away from the corner of the hotel. He put a big rip in the left fender and tore out the headlight. It was hanging out and springing up and down like the eyes you get with those joke-shop glasses.

We passed Ironsides and the Alonzo Wright Bridge and started to climb the mile hill into the mountains.

The train was long gone, following up the river. Too bad we weren't on it.

I was wishing Dad would drive.

"I'll take over later," he said. "It's a new car. He should drive it the first part of the trip. I'll take over at Wakefield." He was talking quietly to me out of the side of his mouth. Frank was concentrating on all the curves the road took to get up to Chelsea.

Frank, the worst driver on the Gatineau.

Luckily there was no traffic coming against us. Frank was going about fifteen miles an hour. He was in the middle of a long coughing and sneezing fit. In the middle of the hill, after the fourth turn, he dropped his cigarette between his legs. For the rest of the hill and the three worst turns he coughed, steered from one side of the road to the other, sneezed, and had one hand underneath himself looking for his lit cigarette. You could smell burning. I wondered what Aunt Dottie would have said.

At the top of the hill was Hendrick's farm where everybody in that huge family was red-headed. You knew you were done climbing when you started to see some red-headed people along the side of the road or leaning on a fence.

"Watch you don't run down a Hendrick," Dad was saying, "you know it's unlucky."

Chelsea was coming up and Dad decided to try and get Frank into King's gas station near there for some gas and a rest. More for the rest than the gas.

We were about six miles from home. Thirty-four to go. It was almost half past three. Dad and I left our place around one. Two and a half hours to go six miles. I was figuring that to be about three miles an hour. A person can *walk* faster than three miles an hour! Just then, Frank turned into King's Station and knocked over a pyramid of motor oil cans near the pumps.

King came running out laughing. ''Frank! I heard you bought a new car! Is this it? She ever a beaut! Look at the nice big teeth! Did you hear about Mean Hughie! I'll believe it when I see it! Come on in the back! I'll get a couple of Hendricks to service your nice new car! Come on Tommy! Come on Frank! Bring young Tommy with you! Would you like a coke? No, no, never mind those cans! I'll get some Hendricks to pick them up! Come on! Come on around the back and have a snort . . . !''

Around behind King's, in Chelsea, Dad got talking more about Mean Hughie. We were sitting on some barrels. I was having another coke. Dad, Frank and King had some snorts of gin.

I was listening carefully to Dad's stuff about Mean Hughie. I was trying to fit Baby Bridget into it all. Frank wasn't listening. He had both eyes closed. He was resting. He must have been pretty tired! Six miles is a long drive!

Specially if you're Frank.

"We were both workin' on the dam," Dad was saying. "Mean Hughie and me, shovelling and pickin' and mixing cement and hammering up forms. And breaking rock. No bellies like now, no flab. Stomachs hard and flat as boards. Six days a week, ten hours a day. And twisting wrists at smoke break. I'd win with the right. Mean Hughie with the left. He was awful powerful in those days. He was about six foot four and weighed around two hundred and twenty pounds and he had a great big head on him and shoulders about this wide. And I remember dinner time with big chunks of homemade raisin bread and green onions big as apples and lots of salt and slabs of fat pork and cold buttermilk from the icehouse. And the dam taking so long and goin' up so slow and everybody on the river above Low, their life going to change forever. They knew it but they didn't really know it. And Mean Hughie living by himself in a cabin he built for himself before he was flooded out and squatted over on the farm where he is now. And his shack, his cabin, was about two hundred yards from the bank of the river. And that's plenty, says Mean Hughie, the water won't come up that far when they slam that dam closed for good. But everybody disagrees with Mean Hughie. Everybody said the water would come way up past his shack. Even the dam man, he came around two or three times and told Mean Hughie that he'd have to move and even offered him money. They took more than five years to put up that dam, so Mean Hughie was about twenty-two then when the dam man made his last visit. Mean Hughie laid him on the sawhorse and rested the bucksaw blade on the dam man's neck and put his left boot up on the dam man's bellybutton and made him say that the water would *not* come up or he would saw off his head.

"No, the water, I promise you, will *not* come up and flood away your nice cabin, Mean Hughie!" says the dam man.

"That's better," says Mean Hughie. "Now you can go."

Dad stopped talking and let everybody laugh for a while.

Even Frank was laughing a bit, in his sleep, about how mean Mean Hughie was and after Dad told some more stuff we woke Frank up and we all got back in the car.

Dad started talking again after we waved goodbye to a whole bunch of red-headed Hendricks and Frank got the car back out on the highway without hitting anything.

Dad didn't know I was interested in Baby Bridget, but he knew I liked his stories so he kept going..

"Now, Mean Hughie's cabin was on deceiving ground. It looked like it was above and back enough from the river, but it wasn't. Most people try to tell Mean Hughie this just about every other day but Mean Hughie isn't listening. He says his shack was there long before they started building the dam and it's a long walk to the water and it's just not going to come up that far. Yes it is, everybody says, you're going to wake up one morning and your bed'll be floating! But they don't like to say it too often to Mean Hughie, or at least not too loud or bold or sarcastic or in a mean way, because they know Hughie will bounce them around the rock pile for a while or deliver them a backhander on the ear which would set your head ringing for about a week. Or worse! Like what happened to Buck O'Connor. Old Buck was acting a bit too frisky around Mean Hughie, talking about his house floating down the river and asking him if his windows were closed and stuff like that. Buck paid for that with one of his ears. Buck was in the middle of saying that Mean Hughie should quit helping to build the dam at Low and go home and build his *own* dam around his house, or take swimming lessons, when Mean Hughie decided to kneel on his chest and cut off a big part of one of his ears with a rusty jack-knife. They say that Buck went right home, looked in the mirror, took a big pair of scissors and snipped off most of his *other* ear just so's he'd look *even!* Anyway old Buck went out West for the harvest that year and never came back."

Just as Dad finished his story about Buck O'Connor's ear, Frank swerved off the road a bit and clipped off a mailbox at the end of somebody's laneway and put a big crack in the right side of our windshield. We were passing the town of Tenaga.

I was thinking that when we got up to Low, if we ever did, Crazy Mickey, my great-grandfather, would be right where he always sat, on the two-seater swing, with my great-grandmother, Minnie, holding hands. She was ninety-nine.

He was a hundred.

I was wishing we were on the train. We'd be almost there by now.

Between Gleneagle and Kirk's Ferry, Frank had a race with a big fat cow with a bell on.

The cow stopped and Frank won the race.

Going past the golf course at Larrimac there was a golfer crossing the road pulling a golf cart.

Frank chased the golfer right up onto the grass on the other side of the road, hit a rock coming down and took our muffler partly off.

The pavement ended around Burnett and instead of following the old road through Cascades and along the river bank, we took the new highway overland through the rock cuts and all that dust and loose gravel and machinery.

We were creeping along about fifteen miles an hour and Dad was singing that turnip song. It was his favourite song. And mine too.

We were about halfway down the mountain into Wakefield and I was wondering if Frank was going to drive into the water and take the river for a while just to get some of the dust off. That would be nice, it seemed to me, to be floating along the Gatineau River in our new Buick with the missing teeth, to trail our hands out the window in the water and cool off, maybe throw in a line and do a little fishing.

But instead of going in the river, we took the turn into Wakefield just as nice as pie. The sun was making diamonds on the Gatineau River water and Dad let out a cheer and took a big suck on his gin bottle and started singing. I'd heard the song a hundred times. And I could hear it a hundred more.

"The place where me heart was
You could easy roll a turnip in;
It was as broad as all Dublin
And from Dublin to the Divil's Glin;
And when she took another sure
She could'a put mine back agin';
Ah Molly's gone and left me here

Alone for to die!
Oh mum dear did ya never hear
Of pretty Molly Brannigan?
Since she's gone and left me, mum,
I'll never be a man agin;
There's not a spot on me hide
That the summer sun will tan agin,
Since Molly's gone and left me here
Alone for to die!''

It was the song about the Irish guy who lost his heart.

The car was making a ticking sound. The fan began pinging on a part of the hood that was bent in.

We drove down the street in Wakefield a bit, beside the empty train tracks and the river and then turned into the yard of the Wakefield Inn. Frank parked the car without running into anything, and we went in.

Another coke!

We talked for a while with some guys about Mean Hughie's cancer and Frank's new car. Some guys went to the window to look at the car and laughed quite a bit.

''We're going to have to do something about Frank's

drinkin'," Dad was saying when Frank was gone to the toilet.

"Take him in and make him take the pledge at the church in Martindale," a big farmer said. He was drinking a quart of Black Horse Ale.

"We might just do that, because his drinkin' is gettin' out of hand altogether," Dad said, and a little later we went into the toilet to get Frank who was asleep in there and then we left.

We drove down the street in Wakefield a bit more and turned into the Chateau Diotte Hotel to find a guy with a crowbar to pry the fan away from the hood of the car.

I had another coke. I went into the bathroom to look in the mirror to see if I was starting to *look* like a coke. Frank and Dad had a large Black Horse each. I took my coke outside and watched a guy with a crowbar pry the hood away from the fan.

"I hear Frank's going to Father Sullivan to take the pledge," the man said, "I'll believe it when I see it!"

"What's the pledge?" I asked.

"It's when you go into the priest's office behind the church and sign a paper swearing to God and the Virgin Mary you'll never touch beer, liquor or wine again, so help you," the man told me.

"I'll believe it when I see it," I said.

Back in the car Dad asked Frank if he'd take the pledge.

"Would you go into the priest's office and take the pledge, Frank?" Dad said to the back seat.

Frank said something about a leak. He was lying down in the back seat with his cheek on his hands.

"We better stop for a leak," Dad said. "Can you wait 'till we get to Alcove? We'll go into 'Chicks' there and have a leak and a bite."

At "Chicks" we had hot chicken sandwiches, a coke and two more large Black Horse Ales. The sandwich made Frank wake up a bit and he started singing "Goodnight Irene" to our waitress. That was his favourite song. Then he fell over backwards off his chair.

It was six o'clock.

"Yes, we definitely have to try and get Frank to take the pledge," Dad said and we left.

We passed right by Farrellton, waved at Father Farrell and didn't stop until we got to Brennan's Hill. We stopped at Monette's Hotel and bought a pail of minnows and some worms.

In Low, we only stopped at two hotels, Doyle's Inn and the Paugan Inn. We were making very good time.

We passed Father Sullivan's church in Martindale with his little bit of paved road outside and got back on the dirt again. We were certainly making very good time. It only took us around six hours in a brand new 1950 car to go about forty miles. A world's record!

Six point six miles an hour!

Could have walked!

Along the road small pigs were walking on tiptoe.

The clouds were like kindergarten cut-outs pasted up there on the blue sky and all piled up like my great-grandma Minnie's white hair on Sunday—and the cows were standing there like wooden statues on somebody's huge lawn and the horses were warm and brown and set up in two's so their heads and tails were together.

It was half past eight when we turned into my grandfather's farmyard.

It was like a photograph, only coloured. Or a painting. For a second everything and everybody was still. All the people were there, in their places, all with their faces turned looking at us in our car. Like a big crowded beautiful colored painting in a museum.

At the back of the painting was the sky and the humpy green mountain. A little closer, there was the river. In the middle was the rolling field. In the front was the farmhouse and the yard and the shed and the big poplar trees and the butternut tree with the evening sun making shade and bright pools of golden light in the yard. And in the yard, the people.

There was Crazy Mickey, my great-grandfather, and his wife Minnie, on their swing. Crazy Mickey, born in 1850. One hundred years old. And Minnie, ninety-nine.

There was Old Tommy, carrying a pail. That was my grandfather, seventy years old, born in 1880.

There was my dad's sisters: Leona, forty-four, at a table washing dishes; Monica, forty-three, drying; Martina, forty-two, pulling wool; Ursula, forty-one, sharpening a knife; Lena, forty, feeding slops to chickens.

There was my dad's brothers: Gerald, thirty-nine, lying on his elbow, smoking; Vincent, thirty-eight, lying on his back, smoking; Joseph, thirty-seven, lying on his side, smoking; Sarsfield, thirty-six, on his stomach, smoking; Armstrong, thirty-five, leaning on the house, lighting up.

And in the very front of the painting, a big crow, flying across, caught for a second, perfectly still.

We got out of the car and Frank leaned on the gate so he wouldn't fall over and everybody was talking at once about Mean Hughie and the cancer and maybe taking Frank to the priest and the weather, but I had my mind on something else.

I was thinking about Baby Bridget.

Soon we would go down to Dad's cabin and set Frank's tent up on the top of the hill and get settled in for the night and then it would be tomorrow and I'd find an excuse to go over to Mean Hughie's farm and see Baby Bridget.

Then I heard somebody say the word "disappeared." Somebody disappeared. Who? Mean Hughie! Mean Hughie has disappeared! About three weeks ago. Gone. Vanished. Just like that. Nobody knows where. Damndest thing.

Mean Hughie.

Gone!

PART
II

My excuse came the very next day.

Dad and I got up early and went up the hill behind the cabin to see how Frank was doing. His tent didn't look as good as it did last night in the dark when we put it up. He must have knocked the main pole out during the night because the tent was flat on the ground and we could see Frank lumping around underneath the canvas.

The trunk of Frank's new Buick was open beside the tent.

"Looks like he took his beer and his outboard motor into the tent with him last night and knocked down the pole," Dad said. "Let's go down and cook up some bacon and eggs. He'll be all right."

Dad and I lit up the outside stove and I went down to the well and got some water. When I got back there was bacon frying. I loved to see the smoke from the chimney of the outside stove moving up through the pine trees and to smell the bacon and the wood.

I put the kettle on.

Dad moved the bacon over and broke four eggs in the deep grease and then moved the pan over to a cool part of the stove and started splashing grease on the eggs with the egg lifter. I took one of the lids off the stove and cooked some toast in the flames with a fork.

I poured the tea and Dad took the hot plates out of the oven.

Then we sat down on the little verandah and had a great big breakfast.

I was mopping up the last of my eggs with some toast when I heard Frank coming down the hill behind us. I knew it was Frank by the thumping. Everybody thumps when they come down the hill, but only Frank would thump like somebody who didn't know if he was walking or running. He thumped right past us and headed down to the river. He was carrying his outboard motor. We watched him go by, but we didn't say anything. We figured Frank didn't want any breakfast. He disappeared for a while and then we could see him again at the shore.

"Have to get that fella to Father Sullivan to take the pledge," Dad said.

We stood up on the little verandah of the cabin to watch Frank down at the river try to put his outboard motor on our boat.

"How about running over to Poor Bridget's and see if she's doing any baking today? Get us a few loaves of nice fresh bread?"

I was thinking about Mean Hughie disappearing and where he might be hiding.

"I'm going to cook up a great big roast of corned beef," Dad was saying, "and we'll have a great big feed of cabbage and corned beef and some nice fresh homemade bread with it for supper.''

Frank, down at the river, had his motor in one hand and was holding out his other hand to keep his balance. He stepped into the rowboat. Now he had both feet in the boat. It was rocking from side to side.

"I'll clean out that great big iron pot and we'll do it all on the outside stove here. I'll pick a great big pail of raspberries when you're gone and get some fresh cream from them up at the farm. And we'll have a great big feed.''

Frank was high stepping it now, and the boat was rocking worse. Now he was towards the back of the boat sort of running.

Now he was over the end of the boat, head first, with the motor in one hand, into the water.

Dad was shaking his head.

"We've got to get him in to talk to Father Sullivan about the pledge,'' Dad said.

"I'll go for the bread,'' I said.

I ran up the hill, passed Frank's tent, cut across Old Tommy's hay field and picked my way carefully through Mean Hughie's slash fence.

A slash fence is made of fallen trees, unlimbed. They're the sloppiest, worst fences in the Gatineau. To make one you just cut down a big tree and leave it there. Then cut another one and leave it there. Do this all the way along and there's your fence. Old Tommy's cows were always getting caught in Hughie's slash fences and sometimes breaking their legs or cutting their stomachs and tearing their bags on the sharp sticks and broken branches in the slash.

I was over on Mean Hughie's land.

I was a bit scared so I started whistling. Mean Hughie has disappeared. Almost three weeks now. Sure. What if he's hiding out in this bush? He could shoot me or jump on me from behind.

The thicker the bush got the more I whistled.

By the time I got to the old logging road, that I remembered from three years before, I was all whistled out. I turned the corner around the barn where I first met Baby Bridget and headed across the yard.

Poor Bridget was baking all right. I could smell it before I knocked on her broken door.

"Young Tommy!" Poor Bridget said, "Holy Mary Mother of God, you've grown like some kind of a lovely weed you have—look at you now. Jesus Mary and Joseph, you're here for bread now and I have lovely bread for you to take home to your father, Tommy. You haven't been here for years, but you're here now and I guess you and your father are stayin' at the cabin and will you be up for a while? Holy bald-headed, here's a chair for you to sit on and rest yourself . . ."

While she was talking and offering me raisins and water a whole lot of kids came peeking and falling into the kitchen through windows and doors and giggling and shoving each other and taking looks at me.

I don't remember what I said when Baby Bridget came in. I think I said hello, but I was trying to swallow at the same time and I sort of choked.

She was hiding her poor arm and looking out through her hair at me with her green eyes. Her mother was still talking.

". . . and Baby Bridget here often asked me about you, the poor darlin' with her poor arm and she . . ."

Baby Bridget turned around to the stove and used the bottom of her dress to open the hot oven door and check on the bread in there.

". . . and you'll stay and wait for this next batch of bread to come out, not this one, for God's sake, but the next one, and you'll sit down with us and have your dinner before you go back to your lovely father with the bread . . . Baby Bridget, get two pails, one for you and one for Young Tommy here and take him down to the berry patch, for the love of God, and get us some berries for dinner while I finish punchin' up this dough . . ."

Baby Bridget and I went to the berry patch across

a creek behind the house. Some of her brothers and sisters tried to follow us, but she gave them a look and they disappeared.

Baby Bridget could pick raspberries faster than I could even though she only had one hand. She'd lean over and hold the berry stem against her stomach with her short arm and pry the berries off the bush with her hand so they'd fall into the pail tied around her waist. She used her fingers on the berries sort of the way you'd tickle a cat underneath the chin.

And her hair fell down like a curtain covering her face when she leaned over.

"It's easier if you tie the pail around your waist," said Baby Bridget.

"What with, a piece of string or something?" I said.

"Binder twine is fine," she said, and then she laughed a bit because of the rhyme she made.

"What's binder twine?" I said.

"It's twine you use in a binder."

She leaned over to start on another bush and then looked up through her hair at me.

"You can't pick berries when you're watchin' somebody else pick berries," she said. I started picking berries like mad.

When my pail was half full I looked up to see how her pail was.

It was full. She was standing there eating what she picked.

Then, I don't know why, but I said this:

"My Aunt Dottie says berries have germs on them."

"Your Aunt Dottie's crazy," said Baby Bridget, and then we went back to her house for dinner.

I felt pretty stupid about the picking berries, but as soon as I got back into the kitchen and all the berries got poured into one bowl I started to forget about it. Then, when Poor Bridget brought out the pot of steaming potatoes and told us all to sit down and the kids started coming out from behind everything to grab the best seats and Baby Bridget kept her hand on the seat beside her to save it for me and told me to sit there, I felt smart again.

I was wondering if they were going to talk about Mean Hughie and all the stuff people were saying about him when Poor Bridget got out the rest of the dinner.

A big bowl of boiled potatoes from the garden with the skins still on, steam coming off them, some of them split, the white showing; a heap of green onions, lying sideways on a plate, the onion part washed but the long green part with mud still on; a platter full of curly pieces of fried pork, the rind still on, the pieces curled up like ears; a loaf of bread and a knife beside it; a big bowl of butter; lots of salt. Plaster the potatoes with butter, put a pile of salt on the oilcloth covering the table beside you to dip your onions in. Pick up the pork with your fingers, one piece at a time, and with your front teeth bite the meat and fat off the rind. Put the rinds in a little pile on the oilcloth on the opposite side of your plate from where the pile of salt is. Get Poor Bridget to cut the bread you want while she holds the loaf against her chest. Eat your crusts.

Eat about four or five potatoes, eight or nine onions, five or six pieces of pork, two slices of bread, lots of salt, lots of butter and leave enough room for two cups of tea and you'll feel good after.

Get your hands sticky with mud and butter and your face covered with pork fat and potatoes. Then burp politely.

Oh, Aunt Dottie! If only you were here to see this!

Poor Bridget didn't sit down at the table with the rest of us. She ate her dinner off the kids' plates and at the stove. She would take a piece of fried pork out of the pan and nibble on it and then come over and feed the rest of it to one of the younger kids. Then she'd take an onion or a piece of potato from one of the other kid's plates who wouldn't eat anything and take a bit of that and then jam the rest of it in that kid's mouth. Then, when she saw another kid eating more than his share, she'd grab whatever he was shoving in his mouth and eat that. And when another kid would slide off his chair under the table, she'd pick up an onion or something, take a bite of it and hand the rest of it under the table to that kid.

And every now and then she'd charge over to the table and flap her apron to get the flies back up in the air.

She was talking about Mean Hughie.

"Their father is gone, did you know? They say they last saw him in the store in Low. Last seen there. Three weeks ago or so. Doctor said he had the cancer. God only knows where he's gone to! Have another potato. How's your father? Is he well? Not sick or anything? Fine man. Their father's gone somewhere. He was a troubled man. God knows he had his troubles. Eat up that pork. There's lots. Have yourself an onion. Yes, he went and disappeared. Just vanished. Gone. A troubled man . . ."

Outside, after dinner, Baby Bridget was standing with me while I wrapped the bread in my shirt.

"Want to see some binder twine before you go?" she said, and took me over to an old falling-down machine shed on the other side of the house.

Inside the door that was hanging on one hinge I could hear pigeons gulping and I could smell machine oil and straw. The sun was rodding through the walls in the gaps between the logs.

The binder sat there like a giant toad. Baby Bridget ducked underneath the raised knives and opened a greasy lid on the side of the machine. Inside there was a big spool of thick string.

"That's binder twine," she said. "It's strong. It comes out of here, through the machine and ties up the oats into sheaves. You can use it for anything. It's very strong. Almost nobody could break that with their bare hands."

"*Almost* nobody?"

She didn't answer. She just looked at me with her green eyes burning.

That night after we had the corned beef and cabbage I asked Dad if it would be all right if I invited Baby Bridget over for supper some night. We were watching Frank trying to clean up the dishes. It seemed like the place got dirtier the more he cleaned.

"Sure," Dad said, "bring her over for supper and I'll make a great big stew and I'll cook a great big raspberry and gooseberry pie. Then we can play cards. Does she like to play cards?"

"I don't know."

"Are you worried about her only having one hand?"

"No. I guess I was wondering if they even *had*

cards at her place. They're awful poor. Maybe she's never played cards.''

"That's all right. We'll show her.''

Frank was trying to dump some slops out the window. But he didn't open the window first so you could say that quite a bit of it wound up on the glass.

"We've gotta get that fella in to see Father Sullivan to take the pledge and quit drinkin','' Dad said.

"I'll believe it when I see it,'' I said.

A couple of days later Baby Bridget came over for supper. We had the stew and cleared off the table to play cards. We didn't get much cards played because we couldn't concentrate.

Frank was cleaning up again.

The floor was covered with soapy dishwater and Frank was slipping and stumbling all over the place and breaking dishes and losing forks under the stove.

It was just as well that Frank was interrupting our game. Baby Bridget was a little shy about the cards because, as she told me later, she'd never played cards before.

Frank was trying to heave out the leftover stew from the big iron pot. Since Dad had cleaned up the window from the last time, Frank decided he'd do it properly and use the door. He gave the screen door a shove so it swung right out and then grabbed the big iron pot and tried to heave out the stew before the door closed. The door was a little faster than Frank was and a lot of the stew got caught in the screen and on the wooden frame. Then Frank looked back to see if anybody was watching (of course we weren't; we were playing cards) and then started to try to clean off the door with the egg lifter. He pushed his face right up close to the stew on the screen and was using the egg lifter to flick off the carrots and peas and stuff. Because Frank was such a good housekeeper, he was opening the screen each time so that what he'd flick would land outside. This made him lean forward. He was concentrating pretty hard on a small chunk of beef or something and leaning further and further forward. Then gravity took over and out the door he went onto his hands and knees. We couldn't see him now, but we could hear him out there grunting and talking to himself and falling down and sliding around on gravy and potatoes on the grass.

"I never put long celery in my stew anymore," Dad was saying, "because there's nothing slipperier than long cooked celery on grass or floors and I also hesitate to put those real small peas in the stew because they stick to a screen door worse than anything."

But later we found out that something sticks to a

screen door even worse than small peas and stew. Coffee grounds. Coffee grounds get right in the little holes in the screen and they're almost impossible to get out. And when they're way up near the top it's even worse.

You see, Frank emptied coffee pots overhand. That's how the grounds got so high on the door. Dad told Baby Bridget that Frank used to be a great baseball player before his head was run over by a tank in the war.

That was the first time I ever heard Baby Bridget laugh out loud.

Suddenly we heard a car horn and Frank started yelling, "Visitors! Visitors!"

Baby Bridget and I went out, stepping over Frank and the stew and ran up the hill to see who it was. It was Gerald driving, Vincent and Joseph in the back, Sarsfield and Armstrong on the running boards, all smoking cigarettes. And it was Aunt Dottie in the front seat! We certainly didn't expect her this soon.

I went over and kissed her ear and told her I was glad to see her. She was sitting on a sheet of white paper in case the seat was dirty. Gerald, Vincent, Joseph, Sarsfield and Armstrong were making a big fuss over her and jabbering away, but she wasn't paying any attention. She was staring at Frank's tent.

"Whose tent is that?" she asked, pointing at it as if it was a big turd or something.

"It's Frank's," I said.

Aunt Dottie got out of the car and asked somebody to get her suitcases out of the trunk. Gerald, Vincent, Joseph, Sarsfield and Armstrong got her suitcases out and piled them around the hood of the car. Aunt Dottie opened one and took out a long pair of rubber gloves and a doctor's mask. Then she took out a pretty big pump spray full of fly tox and some kind of disinfectant.

Then she ordered the boys to go in the tent and throw everything out. Out came Frank's sleeping bag, some shorts, a sweater, a pillow and a bunch of dirty socks. Then his fishing box, and about a hundred bottles of beer and some empty gin bottles.

When it was all out she sprayed everything with her pump gun and then started firing the beer, one bottle at a time, in every direction, as far as she could, down and over the hill into the deepest, thickest wild raspberry bushes.

It took her quite a while, and she was quite puffed out when she was finished.

Then she packed her gloves and her gun and her mask, put a new sheet of white paper on the seat, had the boys put her suitcases back in the trunk and got in the car.

"I will not stay here when that horrible Frank is here! I'll stay at the farm. Drive off!" And away they went.

We looked down the hill where Frank was already crawling around looking for his beer. You could see the bushes moving and hear Frank saying "Ow!" and grunting a bit and talking to himself.

Dad was sitting on the sawhorse.

I said good-bye to Baby Bridget and watched her go up the road and cut through the slash fence.

Later Frank stood up out of the bushes in the evening light. His clothes were torn into long thin strips. He was covered with blood. But he was smiling.

He picked up some bottles in his arms from the pile he made on the grass and headed up the hill to his tent. He had found every single one of his beers.

I went in and got ready for bed. I could hear Frank popping a beer now and then. And I could hear the crickets.

Later the moon came out and Frank was snoring. I went out and looked up the hill. I could see Frank's tent in the moonlight. I thought I could see the sides of the tent moving with the snoring.

The snoring sounded as though someone very cruel was slowly torturing a huge pig.

A few days later I took Baby Bridget fishing. She wasn't as good at fishing as she was at berries.

I put on my bait just right so my hook didn't show and straightened out my leader and checked my spinner and let my line out nice and even and slow until it touched bottom and then raised it up gently a couple of feet and moved it up and down very gently and quietly and then I looked up over the water to the mountain across the river and out of the side of my eye I saw that Baby Bridget was watching me and I laughed and soon after I got a bite and hauled in a nice pickerel. You can't win at fishing when you spend most of the time watching the other guy.

We pulled the boat up on a small sandbar and cleaned our fish on a big white log. Baby Bridget couldn't clean fish because of her arm. But she was good at washing them after they were cleaned. Except the first time. She was swishing our biggest one around in the water and it squirted out of her hand and slid out into the deep water and disappeared.

The sun was hot and the fish blood was bright red on the white log and Baby Bridget was looking at me as though I was going to hit her or something. She was still crouching in the sand with her hand still in the water and she was looking at me as though I was going to go over to her and slap her across the face. Then her eyes filled up with water and the water spilled out and poured down her cheeks.

I told her never mind, it was just an old fish, but it didn't do any good. She just crouched there crying as if she was waiting for me to go over and hit her.

All of a sudden the sun went in and it started to hail. It does that in the mountains around Low, especially on some hot summer days. Before you know it, it's not sunny any more, the wind comes up, a lot of hail is dumped on you and then, all of a sudden, it's over, and the sun is back again.

We waited under a tree and didn't say a word. When it stopped we got in the boat and headed home.

Baby Bridget only said one thing all the way home.

She said this: "Sometimes the hailstones come down as big as walnuts."

I was worried about her, so later I told Dad about it and Dad said that it was probably because Mean Hughie hit her bad one time. He told me that when she had her accident and lost part of her arm, Mean Hughie hit her for getting in the road of the binder. He hit her while the blood was pouring out of her poor arm. I asked Dad how he knew what happened and he said that one of the kids was there and told Gerald, Vincent, Joseph, Sarsfield and Armstrong about it. And they told Old Tommy and Old Tommy told Dad.

And also he said that Mean Hughie broke off a piece of binder twine, with his bare hands, from the machine, and tied Baby Bridget's arm with it so she would not bleed to death.

When I was getting dressed for bed Dad asked if I wanted a little late snack. He had set out some cheese and tea and maybe some pie if I liked. I must have eaten too much because I had a terrible dream.

A man is standing beside a horse. It is Mean Hughie. Mean Hughie is beating the horse with a long black whip. Beating the horse across the back. The horse's eyes are glittering, glistening, shining white and wet, rolling white, flashing, rolling back. Mean Hughie picks a long piece of two-by-four from the wagon and smashes the horse over the back and the skin breaks and the blood comes and the horse pumps his iron back feet, pounds his steel boots into the grey ground and the chains on the traces are jingling and clattering like broken bells.

Someone is yelling.

This is what they're yelling.

"They say Mean Hughie's got the cancer. There's something wrong—Hughie would fill up the whole doorway. But now there's something wrong. What's wrong? The Gatineau's gone. They damned the water. They'd twist wrists 'till their chairs broke. He could drink ten quarts in a night if he had the money. Ten quarts of Black Horse; and eat pickled eggs for a half an hour. One after another steady and then sneeze and blow pickled egg out his nose all over his hands on the table. Pickled eggs and froth and snot all over his sleeves and the back of his big hands on the table. Wait 'till Aunt Dottie hears about this!''

The next afternoon Baby Bridget and I were all set to take a swim when we realized that Frank's tent was surrounded by cows. Somebody left a gate open and the cows were having quite a time licking the tent and eating Frank's socks and shirts that he hung on the front of the Buick to dry.

Baby Bridget and I chased them away and rounded them up to where they were supposed to be in Old Tommy's other field. It took us about an hour and as we were walking past Old Tommy's barn we thought we heard somebody crying inside.

We stopped to listen and sure enough, it was somebody whimpering and crying.

We were still talking about who it might be when we got back to Frank's tent. We stopped to check what the cows had done.

His socks and things he had hung out were lying around and looked like short thick green ropes. The cows had eaten them and then spit them out. They had licked all the windows of his Buick and dropped about a hundred fresh pies all around the tent.

Could make for hazardous footing. Specially if you're stepping out of a tent. Specially if you're Frank stepping out of a tent!

We heard the sound of rustling around inside the tent and then beer opening and some grunting.

We waited to see him come out. Baby Bridget hooked her hand in my arm and we stood there like friends in line for a movie.

Frank stepped out. He had on bare feet and the bright sun closed his eyes. He hit the first cow pie and his leg shot out sideways. His other foot came down to get his balance and hit the second pie. He was running sideways now and pretty well out of control. You could see he was trying to steer himself onto the path through the bushes that went down the hill to the cabin. He was holding his beer up trying not to spill it.

The next two pies did it.

Both feet went straight up in the air and he let out a holler and disappeared, back first, into the raspberry bushes.

Just then, a short distance away, in another part of the berry patch, someone stood up. I could tell by the helmet and all the bug-netting hanging around her face and shoulders and the rubber gloves that it was Aunt Dottie.

She was dumping out the pail of berries she had picked.

"I will not keep berries from the same patch that that horrible Frank has been near! Poisoned! All poisoned!" She picked her way carefully out of the bushes and headed towards the farm.

Then Baby Bridget and I went swimming.

About a week later I sort of told her that I loved her. It came from something Dad told me about Crazy Mickey and Great-grandma Minnie and their swing.

I was sitting on the two-holer with Dad, looking out over the river and the mountain on the other side. When you're in the two-holer you leave the door open so you'll get the breeze. When you're finished you close the door to keep the cows from going in there to lick the seat for the salt and wreck the place. It's opposite from at home. At home when you go into the bathroom, you close the door. Here, you leave it open when you're in there and close it when you leave.

"I heard someone crying in the barn. Someone was sobbing and crying in the barn the other afternoon," I said to Dad.

"It was Crazy Mickey. Every day in the early

afternoon he goes in there and has himself a good cry," Dad said.

"What's he crying about?"

"Most days after dinner Great-grandma Minnie has a little lie down upstairs and Crazy Mickey thinks she's gone away and died somewhere so he goes to the barn and has a good cry. Then he has a snooze and by the time he gets back to the swing, Great-grandma Minnie is all rested and is there on the swing waiting for him. Then he figures she's back from the dead and it's a real miracle and he's so happy to see her he has another good cry."

"This happens every day?"

"Not every day."

"How many times, then?"

"Every day but Sunday. Sunday Great-grandma Minnie doesn't have a snooze after dinner. She doesn't have any dinner. Stays in church all day. Crazy Mickey waits for her outside on the bench."

"Every day but Sunday he thinks his wife died and he feels awful?"

"And every day she comes back and he feels just great."

"Why does he go way over to the barn to cry?"

"Because it was around there that he went to cry when his mother died. He was just a kid then. That'd be about ninety years ago. When they first got here from Ireland.''

"How do you know all this?"

"Because Old Tommy told me."

"How does Old Tommy know?"

"Because Crazy Mickey told *him*. Hand me some of that paper."

"When did people start calling him crazy?"

"He was always called that. Hand me some more of that paper."

"How do you know that?"

"Because Old Tommy told me. Hand me some more of that paper."

"And Crazy Mickey told him?"

"Yep."

"Can you believe someone who's called crazy?"

"Have to."

"Why?"

"Because he's all we've got. I'm going now. Shut the door when you're done."

Anyway, I told Baby Bridget all about it and I said that I thought it was beautiful that they loved each other so much for such a long time.

She didn't say anything, but I could tell what she was thinking. She was thinking it could be us.

Us for that long.

We were out in the boat when I told her that.

It was quiet and clean and slow—just trolling—letting the shore stay just the length of your oar away, chipmunks sitting on the bank watching you slide by, sometimes a porcupine's bum heading up, in a big hurry, going nowhere, waddling away . . .

And rowing, quiet, don't splash the oars, put them in the water each time so there's no splash—watch the little whirlpool that the oar makes run by you, maybe there's a water spider spinning in it, wondering what's happening. And all you can hear is the gurgle sometimes—and maybe a wasp or a dragonfly goes by and makes a small racket, and a bird sings, and you're right under the mountain, in the shade of the mountain there, and you look up, and the mountain and the clouds are moving slowly by, sliding by, and you are still, perfectly still in your little rowboat that doesn't need a motor.

We were trolling down river. I was rowing and Baby Bridget was fishing with a hand line on a stick, a June bug and worms.

We were farther down river than I'd ever been.

We rounded a point, sticking close to the shore. It was evening. I asked Baby Bridget if she wanted to turn back.

"We can go a little more," she said.

We could see the dam in the distance. She had

caught two pike. They were lying in the bottom of the boat, their gills pumping a little bit.

We were getting closer to the dam. Baby Bridget pointed to a little log stable sitting right on the edge of the water near the dam.

"That's where Old Willy the Hummer lives. He's a healer. Some say he's crazy, but he isn't. That's all that's left of his farm. That old stable. He lives there. There's no road to it. You have to go by water."

In the distance you could hear the generators humming.

"Those big cables go right over his shack. It's so noisy there you have to shout."

"You've been there?"

"Yes."

"Why did you go there?"

"He's a healer."

"What were you doing there?"

"I wanted to see if he could make my arm grow back. It was a dumb thing to do."

"What did he do?"

"He said he would heal me someday but in a different way."

"A different way?"

"Yes, a different way, but he wouldn't say any

more. He said I'd know when. And I'd come to him and he'd make me right again.''

"Make you right?''

"Yes, but he wouldn't say any more. Just started humming.''

"Humming?''

"He hums with the humming of the generators. He makes the same sound. I'll take you there sometime. Father Sullivan doesn't like him. He says he's sinning against the church.''

The next day Baby Bridget came over in the late afternoon and we had the cabin all to ourselves. Dad and Frank were gone to Low to the hotel.

I didn't want to play cards and since it didn't look like they'd be back from the hotel until quite late I decided to get out Dad's cookbook and make something fancy for me and Baby Bridget to eat.

We read each other some of the recipes. They were very old.

Then it got dark and I lit the Coleman lamp and we read some more recipes.

Baby Bridget was a good reader. She read me this one twice. It was one of her favourites.

My Mother's Bread Pudding
4 or 5 slices of day-old bread
milk
raisins
brown sugar

Dice up the bread in diced sizes the size of dice.

Put them in a large soup bowl and sort of pat them with the pads of your fingers.

Pour boiling milk over.

Sprinkle with raisins and brown sugar.

With a tablespoon, up in your room, try and eat it, while, downstairs, they're all eating roast beef and laughing.

The one I liked best was this one:

My Father's Fried Potatoes and Eggs
10 potatoes
5 onions
some butter
a bunch of black pepper
lots of salt

Boil the potatoes until they're not quite done.

Let them sit in a bowl in a cool place all night with their coats on.

The next morning, Sunday, when nobody's around, undress them and cut them in irregular shaped, half-a-biteful-sized pieces.

Cut five onions in chunks about the size of dice.

Cover the bottom of a great big black iron pan with 1/4 inch of simmering butter.

Throw in some of the onions.

After a while, throw in some more onions and darken the whole surface with a thick dark mist of pepper.

After another while throw in the potatoes and the rest of the onions.

Lash the salt to it and crank up the heat.

For quite a while keep turning the whole thing with an egg flipper or something. Clang the side of the pan with the egg flipper, violently, making the pan ring, if you can, like a church bell. Do this until everything is brown.

Turn off the heat; cover for the time it takes you to drink one pint.

Forget the eggs.

But the one we made was this one:

My Father's Onion Sandwich

2 huge Spanish onions
fresh bread
butter
salt
beer
mayonnaise

Cut the middle slice (1/2" thick) out of each onion. Throw the rest of both onions out in the yard.

Get a big loaf of fresh, hot, homemade bread from some farmer's wife whose dress smells like milk.

Cut 2 slices, (2" thick) from the centre of the loaf.

Save the rest of the bread for tomorrow's bread pudding.

Plaster the bread with butter.

Put on the onion slices.

Pour salt to her.

Get a beer and some mayonnaise.

Put lots of mayonnaise on the onion slices.

Close the sandwich and with the heel of your hand, press.

Eat.

It was quite a romantic evening.

A couple of nights later we were up at the farm, all sitting around Old Tommy's kitchen talking about Mean Hughie. There was Crazy Mickey and his wife Minnie in their rockers in the corner by the stove. There was Old Tommy, fixing a pail at the table. There was Leona shucking peas in a big dish. There was Monica throwing the shucks out the screen door for the chickens in the morning. There was Martina pulling wool. There was Ursula sharpening a knife. There was Lena, sewing.

There was Gerald at the door, smoking; there was Vincent having a smoke at the table with Joseph who was doing the same; there was Sarsfield with his feet up on a stool, smoking; and there was Armstrong, scratching a match on his boot, lighting up.

And there was Aunt Dottie in front of the stove with one of the lids opened part way. You could see the fire glowing a bit through the space.

A little fire at night, just to take the chill off.

Aunt Dottie was wearing a gauze mask over her nose and mouth, tied behind her head with a snow-white lace.

On a stool in front of her there was a little saucer of honey. She was holding a very dainty, pretty little pink flyswatter in one hand and a tissue all ready in the other.

When a fly would light on the stool to investigate the saucer of honey, she would snick it with her little swatter, wrap it in the tissue and it would wind up in the fire just slick as a button.

What a way to go!

Baby Bridget and I were listening to what they were all saying about Mean Hughie. We were sitting in the corner on a bench.

Dad was down in the cabin having a snooze and Frank was gone out to Low in his car.

"They say they saw Mean Hughie at the store in Low charging up a lot of flour, salt, sugar, lard, baking powder and shotgun shells," Old Tommy was saying. "He bought it all right, but he never came home with it. Poor Bridgit never saw him again. That was over a month ago. Nobody's seen him since."

"They say he's gone somewhere to die of his cancer," Leona said. She was handing Monica some shucks. Monica opened the screen door and threw the shucks out in the yard. Not one of them hit the screen. When the door closed I noticed something I had never noticed before. When the moon shines through a screen and you're looking through the screen at the moon you can sometimes see a cross. When you take away the screen the cross is gone.

"Mean Hughie's vanished," said Gerald.

"Gone," said Vincent.

"Disappeared," said Joseph.

"Thin air," said Sarsfield.

"Melted away," said Armstrong.

"There's quite a cross on the moon tonight," Crazy Mickey was saying to Minnie.

"Mother of God," said Minnie, "Mother of God."

"Did you see there's quite a cross on the moon tonight?" Crazy Mickey said. "They say when the cross is on the moon, our Holy Mother is nearby."

"Jesus Mary and Joseph," said Minnie.

"He thinks the cross on the screen is real," I said right close to Baby Bridget's ear.

"Shh," said Baby Bridget.

"Mean Hughie's gone and disappeared," said Gerald.

"Up and gone," said Vincent and Joseph.

"Vanished into thin air," said Sarsfield.

"Nowhere to be found," said Armstrong. "They say Mean Hughie is nowhere to be found!"

We were all quiet for a while just listening to the boys smoking and the peas being shucked and the knife being sharpened and the rockers rocking.

And the flies dying.

Then we heard a crunching sound outside. The sound of Frank coming up nice and easy in his car into a tree.

Frank was back from Low.

Gerald, Vincent, Joseph, Sarsfield, Armstrong, Baby Bridget and I went out to see.

Frank's car was up against Old Tommy's big butternut tree. There was some steam floating up. It looked pretty in the moonlight.

Baby Bridget walked me part way home and then cut across the slash fence to her place.

I called to her before she disappeared out of the moonlight into the bush.

"They say they're soon going to take Frank in to Father Sullivan to take the pledge!" I called.

I heard her laugh a very nice laugh from the bush where she had just disappeared. I think I heard her say, "I'll believe it when I see it."

I went home to the cabin and went to sleep.

The next day we went swimming early and then lay down on the big rock beside where the boat was tied up. The sun was nice and warm and I had my chin on my hands and I was watching the water on my eyelashes making rainbow colours in the light.

All of a sudden I noticed, right in front of my face on the rock, that a dragonfly was just starting to stick his head out of the bug he was living inside of. He had crawled up from under the water and picked a warm place on the rock right where I was lying to dry himself out and crawl out of his skin and then take off. His head was out and I could see him moving his shoulders to come out farther. Next, I knew, he'd spring his long tail out and dry off his big wings. Then he'd leave.

It would take a long time.

Baby Bridget and I lay on the rock on our stomachs facing each other and watched him working his way out.

The dragonfly was between our faces.

Everything was quiet until I heard some thumping on the hill.

It was Frank coming down with his motor again. My mind started working. I knew he was going to come down and ruin everything. I knew he was going to come up on the rock to see what we were doing and probably drop his motor in the water or step on our dragonfly or make so much noise trying to get in the boat that a thunderstorm would come up and our fly would think it was the end of the world and quit right there.

Or he'd sit down with his legs apart and let his testicles hang out of his bathing suit and embarrass everybody and ruin everything.

I knew it.

But I was wrong.

He did something even worse.

Part way down the hill he stopped and put down the motor right in a gooseberry bush. Then he stood there, with his hand over his eyes, watching us. He was swaying quite a bit and I thought he was going to fall all the way down the hill and we'd have to get up and help him all the way up and by that time everything would be spoiled.

But he didn't.

What he did was he started shouting.

"Love!" he shouted.

He was shouting "love!" standing there, shouting "love!" and you could hear it echo all over the Gatineau River from the mountain and back again.

"Love! There's love here! Love!"

Then he turned around and staggered back up the hill to tell Dad.

"Love!" he shouted and the echo came back. "Love. Come and see it! There's love here! Love! Love!"

I heard the screen door slam and I knew that it was Dad, coming out to see what all the racket was. Then we heard Frank start his song.

> "Irene Goodnight,
> Irene Goodnight,
> Goodnight Irene,
> Goodnight Irene,
> I'll see you in my dreams."

Frank was doing his pitti-pat, pitti-pat on his pot.

Dad had him by the arm. They were standing there looking at us looking at the dragonfly.

Then Dad shouted down the hill.

"Today's the day. Today's the day we go to see Father Sullivan with you know who!"

"I'll believe it when I see it!" I said. "I'll believe it when I see it!"

We waited around for a while, but the sun went in and the dragonfly decided to wait so we went up the hill to see what was going on.

Dad was dragging Frank up to the car.

"We'll pick up some of the boys at the farm to give us a hand!" Dad said and we helped him get Frank into the car.

We picked up Gerald, Vincent, Joseph, Sarsfield and Armstrong, and the car was so full of people and cigarette smoke by the time we got to the church at Martindale that when we opened the doors to get out, I'm sure the people around, if they were watching, thought the car was on fire.

We got Frank out of the car and everything was pretty smooth until we got to the door of Father Sullivan's office at the back of the church.

Frank was holding on to the door frame with one hand. He had a pretty good grip on it and it looked like we weren't going to get him in there.

Father Sullivan was yelling at us, telling us what to do.

"Push his arse, lads! Push his arse!" shouted Father Sullivan.

Gerald, Vincent, Joseph, Sarsfield and Armstrong were pushing Frank pretty hard and Frank was starting to lose. Then all of a sudden he reached back with his other arm and grabbed the other side of the door frame. Now he had a good grip with both hands and it was starting to look like Frank just wasn't going in there.

Then Father Sullivan solved the problem. He went around the side of the church and came back with two big rocks. One for me and one for him.

"We'll hit him on the knuckles with these rocks," said Father Sullivan. "You hit him on *that* hand, Young Tommy, at the same time as I rap him one on this hand. Nice and hard now. It'll be good for him. And don't worry. We do this all the time."

Father Sullivan had his rock right over his head in both hands so he must have brought it down on Frank's knuckles a lot harder than I did.

Anyway, Frank let go in a hurry and Gerald, Vincent, Joseph and Armstrong (there was no room for Sarsfield) ran him into the priest's little office and into the chair.

We waited outside for about fifteen minutes and by the time Frank came out, quite a little crowd had gathered. When Frank appeared carrying his piece of paper that Father Sullivan made him sign saying he would never touch Beer, Liquor or Wine again so help him God and the Virgin, everybody started to clap and cheer a bit.

Frank was studying the paper and swaying there in the sunlight.

"He's lookin' for loopholes," Dad said and we helped Frank into the car and drove back to the cabin.

PART
III

That night after Dad and I had some leftover stew (he gave me the last carrot), we went to bed and I went right to sleep thinking about the dragonfly.

But I didn't dream of the dragonfly.

I dreamt of Mean Hughie. It wasn't like the dream I had before.

Mean Hughie is very small and away down in a well or a hole and I am looking down to him and he is crying out for help, but there is no voice, no sound, just his mouth opening and closing.

Then, away across the river, I can see two hands, gripping the top of the huge mountain like somebody's hands on a fence. I know they are Mean Hughie's hands. I can see the hair standing up on the knuckles and the scars and the black fingernails. The hairs on his knuckles are like pine trees. Then the top of his greasy hat rises slow over the mountain, blocking out the sun, and then Mean Hughie's huge face, the forehead, eyes and nose of Mean Hughie, looking at me between his hands, staring right at me from up over there, over the mountain, about a mile away!

I am screaming but I can't hear myself because of the wind that comes up, making the river black, and because of the thunder rolling around. My mouth opens and shuts, opens and shuts, but no sound comes.

Only the wind screaming through the pine trees and the thunder rolling.

What if Mean Hughie's shoulders and his chest come next and then one knee, as he climbs over the mountain and steps into the river? Then up to his thighs in water he takes two wading steps and wades deeper until the water is up to his chin and then over his head, just his hat showing? Then, what if suddenly the water bursts open and up our hill comes Mean Hughie, water running from his clothes and slime and weeds and fishing lines and wagon wheels and farm wreckage left from the flood sticking to his pants and boots and grabs me like you'd grab a bird with a broken wing and tears the legs off my body like I once tore the legs off a grasshopper? I scream and scream but my mouth is only opening and nothing is coming out . . .

When I woke up Dad was holding me in his arms.

I was yelling something about Mean Hughie.

"It's all right. It's all right," Dad was saying patting me and holding me in his big arms.

"Everything's all right. Everything's all right."

"I saw Mean Hughie come over the mountain!"

"Just a bit of a dream," Dad was saying and then he went and got me a cup of water.

I lay there for a long time staring up at the rafters of the cabin.

Then I got up and got dressed.

I went outside.

Dad was asleep and Frank was snoring up a storm in his tent up the hill. Across the river, the moon was sitting there over the mountain like a cut fingernail. The clouds were moving heavy past it, silver and black. There was a steady wind.

I had the feeling that something was going to happen. I could feel it in my stomach. I went up the hill, past Frank's tent, and looked out over the field towards the farmhouse and the road. The moon was spilling a little light from between the black mountain onto the field and the dirt road.

Then I saw a figure coming down the road towards me. I knew right away it was Baby Bridget. I walked up the road to meet her halfway. Before we reached each other she started talking.

"I've got to see the Hummer. The time is now. I can feel it. Will you take me? He's going to heal me. I know it."

"Now? Tonight?"

"Now."

"Row down there in the dark?"

"There's just enough moon."

There was a silence while two crickets talked to each other out in the field.

I got two old sweaters out of the cabin without waking Dad and we picked our way down the hill, through the raspberry bushes and the moonlight, to the boat.

I rowed. Baby Bridget sat sideways, the way she always did when she trolled, but this time there was no trolling. She was thinking and thinking hard.

It's funny, but if you like somebody, a girl say, you can tell what they're doing, even if you can hardly see them. I knew Baby Bridget had a lot on her mind.

My right oar had one squeak in it each time I pulled it back. It was the only sound except for the gurgling of the water. The steady breeze was warm and going with us. The mountains on each side of us moved by as slow as boats, huge and black.

I started to sing in time with my friend the squeak. I sang Dad's favourite.

> "The place where me heart was
> You could easy roll a turnip in;
> 'Twas as broad as all Dublin
> And from Dublin to the Divil's glin;
> And when she took another sure
> She could'a put mine back again;

Oh Molly's gone and left me here,
Alone for to die.''

My hands were getting a little stiff by the time we rounded the point. It was a long row. We could see the lights of the dam and the power plant twinkling up ahead. They looked pretty.

You couldn't hear the generators humming yet.

"When you came here before, how did you get here?" I was wondering how she could have rowed with her arm the way it was.

"I walked in from Low. I walked over the mountain and climbed down the cliff beside the dam. But it's a bad way to go. It's too hard. I almost fell. Hummer took me back out by boat."

We could hear the generators now. The lights weren't twinkling any more. They were staring. Beady little eyes. Not pretty any more.

We tied up to Hummer's little broken-down dock. His door was only a few feet from the water. The humming was so loud now that when I asked Baby Bridget one more question I couldn't hear my own voice. My mouth moved, but the humming swallowed up what I said.

Baby Bridget pushed open his door and we went in. It was an old stable fixed up inside. The breeze from the open door flickered the candles and made the whole place move. There were candles all over the room. In the corner there was a statue of the Virgin Mary with a candle burning before it. In the other corner there was a small altar with a crucifix and about a dozen candles that you pay a quarter to light for people's souls in church. There was a table in the middle of the room covered with candles in different shapes, the flames all burning and flickering, making the whole room dance with many shapes of shadows. There were candles on the stove and on an old barrel in the other corner. There were candles burning in the small window. Hanging from chains from the ceiling there were candle pots, all their candles burning, making the ceiling move with lights and shadows.

The humming from the dam was so deep and strong you could feel it in your feet and up your legs.

On one side of the room there was a ladder, leading up to a loft.

Coming backwards down the ladder, there was a man. A little wee man with a voice like thunder.

"BABY BRIDGET! BABY BRIDGET! YOU'RE NOT TOO LATE! GO TO MEAN HUGHIE TONIGHT! TONIGHT!"

He was bent over and wizened. He was standing beside me feeling my arm. He was bony and hump-backed. His teeth were black and his mouth wrinkled and his little ears were full of hair. He was feeling my arm with his skinny hand.

"YOUR FRIEND IS STRONG! HE'LL TAKE YOU TO MEAN HUGHIE! UP RIVER AT THE OLD RAMSAY PLACE! HE'S THERE! THERE YOU WILL BE HEALED! HEALED! YOUR FRIEND IS STRONG! HE WILL TAKE YOU!"

Then old Willy the Hummer started moving around his room. Humming.

If you're standing beside a machine, a furnace or a fridge or a motor or something, and you hum the same note the machine is humming, you can feel the vibrations; you feel like the machine and you are the same. The sound fills your whole head.

He was kneeling in front of the statue of the Virgin, humming with the dam.

"M M M M M M M M M M M M M M M M M M M M M! HOLY MARY MOTHER OF CHRIST!

M M M M M M M M M M M M M M M M M M M M M M!"

The sound filled the room, my whole body, the world. I put my hands over my ears. But it didn't do any good. It was just the same inside me as out.

"M M M M M M M M M M M M M M M M M M M M M!"

He was sprinkling holy water around the room from a small bowl.

"M M M M M M M M M M M M M M M M M M M M M!

EVERYTHING CHANGES! EVERYTHING CHANGES! YOU CAN'T STEP INTO THE SAME RIVER TWICE! MEAN

HUGHIE IS CHANGING! CHANGING VERY FAST! YOU
HAVEN'T MUCH TIME! HUM M M M M M M M M M M
M M! HUM! HUM WITH THE POWER! EVERYTHING
CHANGES! YOU CAN'T STEP IN THE SAME RIVER TWICE!
GO TO HIM BRIDGET! GO TO MEAN HUGHIE! THERE IS
HEALING THERE! AT THE OLD RAMSAY PLACE!''

He was putting oil on our foreheads with his thumb.
Crosses of oil on our foreheads.

Next thing I knew we were outside. We were
looking up at the power cables swinging over Hummer's place across the moon. They were buzzing and
humming right in tune with old Willy.

I was feeling strange and dizzy, and Baby Bridget
had me by the hand.

The Hummer held the nose of the boat while we
got in. His voice blended with the dam and we pulled
away.

I was rowing like mad.

The lights stopped staring and started twinkling
again.

The sound faded.

We were back to the squeak of the oar when I
stopped rowing to get my breath. I put on one of the
old sweaters and Baby Bridget draped the other one
over her shoulders.

She looked beautiful in the moonlight.

I asked her the question that she didn't hear me ask before at Old Willy's dock.

"How did he get to live there? There's no road. Why is he there?"

"He's there because that's what's left of his farm. A long time ago, before the water came up, he had a nice farm there. My mother told me. Old Tommy told *her*. Hummer stayed. His whole farm was flooded and washed away except his upper stable at the top of his last field. The road, everything. He stood at his last door and prayed the water would stop. It did. He stopped the water."

"Why did you go to him in the first place?"

"Because he's Mean Hughie's half brother. He's sort of my uncle. He knows all about Mean Hughie."

I was leaning on my oars and staring at the shadow of Baby Bridget. My mind was spinning. I was thinking of all her sadness.

"Can you start rowing soon? We have to hurry. Old Willy said there wasn't much time," she said softly to me.

I knew where the old Ramsay place was. It was about two miles farther up river than Dad's cabin. I'd been there a few times hunting blueberries with Dad. There were some abandoned farm buildings and some dead machinery. It was on the other side of the river. It was the loneliest place I'd ever been.

Dad said there were ancestors of the farm animals there, gone wild. Wild pigs and cats and chickens and dogs. Ancestors.

But I never saw any.

I could feel my strength bulging.

I started rowing.

Not fast but long and hard.

The breeze was against us and so was the water. The moon was most of the way across the sky now. I could feel the blisters starting on my hands. We were passing Dad's cabin. We couldn't see it because there was no light on but I could tell where it was by the shape of the shore and the mountains.

I was thinking about Mean Hughie. Was he really there like old Hummer said?

The breeze was now more like a small wind.

I started humming the Heart Song.

"What's that song mean? That song you were singing. About the heart?" Baby Bridget asked.

"The place where me heart was
You could easy roll a turnip in?"

It's Dad's song. He got it from old Tommy. Old Tommy got it from Crazy Mickey," I told her.

"Where did Crazy Mickey get it from?"

"From Ireland. He came here when he was ten. That was ninety years ago."

"Way before the dam came."

"Must have been nice here then."

"People must have been happy then," said Baby Bridget.

My hands were getting pretty sore. Baby Bridget put her feet against mine for support to make my rowing easier. It was good to talk and take my mind off the pain.

"The song is about a man who lost his heart. The hole where his heart used to be was so big you could roll a turnip in it. And the hole got bigger. It was as big as the city of Dublin. Even bigger. It was as big as the space between Dublin and Hell. It's a sad song. Dad sings it when he's drinking. He sings it a lot around Christmas, too. It's not a Christmas song, but he seems to sing it around Christmas anyway."

I stopped talking and I could tell Baby Bridget wasn't in the mood for a story because she didn't laugh or say anything or even sigh. She just pressed her feet harder against mine to help me row.

The only noise now was the oar squeaking and the water slurping around the boat. We were getting close to Ramsay's Point. I looked behind me and I could see the shadow of the point humping out into the water. The light from the little moon made a needle in the water right against our boat.

The moon and the needle followed and watched every move we made.

We rounded the point and rowed into the bay. Just before the moon went behind the point we saw the shadow of the broken dock at Ramsay's Landing. It looked like a giant grasshopper that had come to the water to drink, and drowned there, his back legs and part of his body still on the shore, his head under water.

We ran the boat up on the grasshopper's back and tied the rope on one of his jumping legs.

We walked up the clay bank and followed the trail into the black tunnel the trees made. We had no moon now and Baby Bridget took my hand and we felt along the road with our feet.

The steeper the path got the more we stumbled and felt our way. I was just going to say something about being lost when I could see a grey hole up above us. Some light. We headed for it and soon we could almost see the road we were on.

We could hear some pig noises and some running in the bush. Wild ancestors of the Ramsay pigs.

We came out of the tunnel into a clearing. Maybe the sun was somewhere. It was coming on morning.

Everything was getting grey as we followed the path across the clearing.

Soon we could see some buildings, small against a rock cliff, outlines of buildings, falling down slowly. The Ramsay buildings, dead buildings, falling over, and machinery, lying there in the tall grass, wheels up, curving rusty iron, pain in the grass, dead bodies of machinery, a binder upside down, in the tall grass, a rusted hayrake in the grass.

Close to the buildings now.

There's dew on the path grass.

We see, beside one of the buildings, a long box.

And maybe something or somebody getting into the box.

The sky gets lighter.

We see that the box is like a coffin.

A coffin, not falling down like the buildings, but straight and strong. It's made of old wood, but it's not falling over. It's straight and strong.

We reach the coffin and look in.

It's Mean Hughie in there.

Poor Mean Hughie. He looked so pitiful. His eyes were big and his face was bony and his hair was almost gone except for little patches every now and then. His cheeks were sucked right in and his teeth were showing like he was grinning, but he wasn't.

He put his hand on the side of the coffin to pull

himself up. He wanted to lean on one elbow. His shirt was open down the front and coming off his shoulders. His arms were like sticks and his shoulders were smooth as driftwood.

He had one knee raised; it was a smooth white ball showing through the rip in his pant leg. His hand, holding on to the side of the coffin, was like a claw.

His chest was bumpy and glistening white and you could almost see through him. The veins in his neck were pumping with his heart.

He had made his own coffin and then climbed into it.

He was trying to die.

His coffin was made of slab wood and barn boards. The frame was made of grey two-by-fours from the rack of the old hay wagon. It was away too big for him now. He made it to fit himself before the cancer got going faster in him and made him so small and light and thin.

I had the feeling that I could have reached down and lifted him out like a long bony baby.

And when he spoke his voice was so small it sounded as if he was talking over a telephone while you were holding the receiver away from your ear.

"I shouldn't have hit you that time you lost your poor arm," he said with his tiny voice.

His voice was so small that he sounded as if he

were away down in the bottom of a well somewhere. Away down in the bottom of a mine shaft somewhere.

"I shouldn't have hit you that time you lost your poor arm," the voice said.

Then, like somebody way inside a cave somewhere or someone on the other side of a dam, the voice, again.

"I'm sorry, Baby Bridget."

Baby Bridget put her ear closer to Mean Hughie's lips to make sure she heard.

"I'm sorry, Baby Bridget, I was so mean."

Baby Bridget looked at me through her hair. She was asking me with her eyes if I was listening. Did I hear what Mean Hughie was saying? Did I hear the same thing that she heard?

I leaned over the side of the coffin a little more. Mean Hughie was too weak to hang on to the side with his claw anymore. He let his head back down.

"I'm sorry for what I done to you, Baby Bridget." His voice was as thin as paper. Baby Bridget leaned over and put the stub of her short arm near her father's hand. His fingers felt it and they curled around it and he groaned. He closed his eyes and stroked her arm, petted her arm with his fingers.

Then, Baby Bridget, in the nicest, most gentle,

soft voice I ever heard, the kindest voice, the most forgiving voice I ever heard, answered.

"It's all right, Pa," she said, she whispered, she breathed the words close to her father's ear.

"It's all right, Pa.

"It's all right, Pa."

I got up and moved over to a stump quite a ways away so they could be alone. It was getting to be a beautiful morning. The sun was shining right through the cracks between the logs of Ramsay's old house. A couple of chipmunks were chasing each other somewhere in the bush.

Old Hummer had said there was healing here. Old Hummer said Baby Bridget's friend was strong. I was the friend.

Strong?

What could I do? I knew her arm wouldn't come back. I knew she would be disappointed. I knew she would get up off her knees after a while and turn around and her arm would be exactly the same.

Strong?

There was nothing strong I could do. All I could do was sit there and watch. A big crow called out from the top of one of the knotty pines. I looked up and spotted him. He called again. How lucky he is, I thought. Up there, away from everything, fly away whenever he wants.

"I know, old crow," I said up to the crow, "that there'll be no healing going on here." I must have been pretty exhausted, talking to crows.

I looked down again and saw Baby Bridget standing up beside Mean Hughie's coffin. Everything was quite hazy because my eyes were full of the bright blue sky behind the crow.

She was walking towards me.

I could tell that Mean Hughie was dead.

I was trying to focus my eyes to see if her arm had grown back. I knew it was a stupid hope to have, but I couldn't help having it. I was feeling more sorry for her than I ever felt about anything before.

Her arm came into focus.

It was the same as before.

I was trying to think of something smart to say. Something that would make her feel good. Tell her a Frank story maybe. No. Sing a little bit to her maybe. No. Throw a rock at the crow. No.

"He said he was sorry he was so mean," she said to me, looking right at me, her eyes full of water.

"He said he loved me and he was sorry." Her eyes were big with water, but she looked good. She had a nice look on her. It wasn't a happy look. But it was a kind of nice look.

Then all of a sudden I knew. I knew what that crazy old Hummer meant. Healing.

Healing. There *was* healing. But it wasn't her arm that got the healing. No. Not the arm.

It was the heart.

The heart got healed.

Baby Bridget's *heart*!

We went down into the gully in the shade where the creek ran through the Ramsay place and picked a lot of cool green ferns and brought them up and put them quietly on top of Baby Bridget's pa in his coffin. Then we went down into the gully and got some more.

Baby Bridget picked some daisies and some barley from Ramsay's old front field and sprinkled them over the ferns to make it pretty.

I saw a wild ancestor chicken run out of the bush and run back in again.

The crow called from his lookout and then flew off.

"We'll take Pa home," Baby Bridget said.

I was already looking around for some way to get the coffin down the steep old road to the river. Behind the house I found the Ramsay's wooden stone-boat. It was a big wooden sleigh they used to pile rocks on. They'd pile rocks on it and the horses would pull it out of the field. Then when they used their mowers and binders their fields would be clean and the wheels wouldn't get caught in the rocks.

They worked hard, those Ramsays, so they could live.

I found a length of rusty chain beside a dead plough and lashed it onto the iron bar across the front of the stone-boat and towed the stone-boat over to the coffin.

The wood that Hughie made his coffin out of was very old and very dry but it was still pretty heavy.

I lifted one end of the coffin on to the stone-boat and then the other end.

"Your friend is strong. He will help you!" I could almost hear the Hummer saying it. I could feel my muscles in my arms and legs. Baby Bridget was watching me.

I stepped inside the chain so that it was around my waist and started to pull.

I was strong.

Strong as a horse.

I dragged the stone-boat with the coffin on it across the long grass of the meadow to the place where the old road took off down the mountain.

It didn't look like a tunnel now. Everything was bright. The sun was making quick shadows on the old road and the drop didn't look so steep.

And all the birds were singing their beaks off.

And Baby Bridget with the healed heart held Mean Hughie's coffin with her hand.

Half way down I had to get out of the chain, turn around and hold the load so it would slide easy and not get out of control.

We came down the clay bank to the grasshopper's back and sat down to rest.

Baby Bridget put her feet in the water.

I studied our next job.

We had to put the coffin in the boat and row Mean Hughie down the river. The coffin wasn't as long as the boat, but it was too long to fit any other way except across the gunnels in front of me, leaving enough room for me to row and balance the weight a bit.

I got back in the chain and waded into the water up to my waist, pulling the coffin until the end was wet. Then I pulled the boat alongside the end of the coffin and got Baby Bridget to go into the water and put her weight on the middle of the boat with her armpits.

I lifted one end of the coffin onto the side of the boat and slowly nudged it over until it was balanced nice and even across the back half with enough room for me to row. Then I swung the boat around so the bow was on shore and I got in and sat at the oars.

Baby Bridget got in behind me and sat on the little bow seat. It was enough balance.

I backed off the shore and turned around and headed out of the bay into the main channel. The daisies and barley and ferns on top of Mean Hughie were moving a bit in the breeze.

I could hear a small plane buzzing above us somewhere. I looked up, but I couldn't find him. We must have looked strange to him. We were shaped like a cross. A cross rowing down the big river. I wondered what Crazy Mickey would think. A cross rowing down the river!

We rounded the point and came into the main channel. The wind there was bigger and I concentrated on keeping the boat balanced, using the coffin as a kind of sail. We were moving pretty fast now and I was working hard with the oars so we wouldn't get out of control. As long as the wind was right behind us, blowing the way we were going, we were all right. We were starting to get some whitecaps and I looked back to see if Baby Bridget was all right, when I heard a popping noise. It was a noise like someone had dropped a walnut from away up, and it hit the boat and bounced out again. I turned back and heard another one. Then I saw what it was.

They weren't walnuts dropping into the boat. They were hailstones. The sun had gone out and there was a big deep black cloud sitting right over us. Up ahead I could see the water go dark and I could hear a hissing sound.

Then it hit us. The hailstones were bouncing off the boat and off our heads straight back up in the air.

I looked back. Baby Bridget had her arms over her head and her head down between her knees.

It was like someone was dumping buckets and barrels of walnuts on us. They were zinging into the water and bouncing off the bottom of the boat and the seats and thumping into the daisies and barley and ferns on top of Mean Hughie.

The boat started to swing and the wind was acting crazy. I knew it would only last a few minutes. I didn't want to fight the wind, just go with it until it settled down again.

We started turning.

We started turning, spinning, and I worked the oars so we would do just what the wind wanted.

We were spinning faster and faster and the coffin started to slide off and pull the boat over to one side. I shifted my weight to try to hold on, but we were out of control.

I knew we were going over and I looked back at Baby Bridget. She still had her head on her arms.

The next thing I knew we were in the water.

I came up and grabbed on to the side of the coffin. I couldn't see the boat or Baby Bridget anywhere.

I worked my way around the other side of the coffin.

Then I saw her arm come out of the water and I heard some shouting.

I helped Baby Bridget grab on to the coffin with her good arm. She was coughing a bit, but she was all right. Then I heard the shouting again. There was a boat somewhere. It sounded like Dad.

The hail quit as fast as it started and I could see a couple of boats and I could hear some oars squeaking.

It was Dad and Gerald in one boat, and Vincent and Joseph in another boat, and Sarsfield and Armstrong in another one.

I pushed Baby Bridget up into Dad's boat and Joseph helped me into his boat.

Sarsfield and Armstrong tied a rope to the coffin. They both had wet cigarettes in their mouths.

The wind settled down and the clouds disappeared.

"Hummer told us where you went," Dad was saying. "He told us you went to find Mean Hughie. So we took off to find you."

I looked at Baby Bridget. She was watching Mean Hughie's coffin being towed behind the other boat.

The ferns and barley and daisies were all gone and

Mean Hughie was floating nice as pie inside his coffin. Each time the oars pulled, his head would hit the end of the coffin a little bit.

It wasn't funny. I wouldn't say it was funny. But it wasn't sad or horrible either. It was just kind of peaceful and restful looking.

We rounded the point and pulled in beside the big rock at Dad's cabin where we had watched the dragonfly. The day was being nice again and there was a bit of a crowd on the shore.

There was also a fire with a tub boiling on it. Aunt Dottie was poking in the tub with a stick, and there was lots of steam.

We got on shore.

Everybody was talking about what happened. Crazy Mickey and Minnie were there holding on to each other and Father Sullivan walked into the water and kneeled beside Mean Hughie's coffin. Hummer was there shouting something to the sky and Leona and Monica were knitting and Martina and Ursula and Lena were spreading some clothes on bushes to dry.

Gerald, Vincent, Joseph, Sarsfield and Armstrong went up the hill to get a wagon to take Mean Hughie to the churchyard at Martindale.

And Frank was there.

Frank was there in his bathing suit with the usual hanging out, drinking some very green stuff out of a bottle. He was singing "Irene Goodnight" and drinking this green liquor out of a bottle with a long neck and a fat bottom.

"What about the pledge?" I said to Dad. "Didn't he promise not to drink beer, liquor or wine ever again?"

"Yes he did," said Dad. "But that's not beer, liquor or wine. That's Creme de Menthe. That's not beer, liquor or wine. That's what you call a *liqueur*. I told you he'd find a loophole. He went into Low this morning and bought a case of it!"

"And what's Aunt Dottie doing?" I asked.

"She's boiling clothes."

"Boiling clothes?"

"Frank's clothes. She's boiling them."

PART
IV

Later that day I ended up at Baby Bridget's. There was nobody else around. Just Baby Bridget and me.

She said she wanted to show me something in the machine shed.

I was shaking inside like a poplar leaf. We were standing in the machine shed beside the same binder that cut off her arm. The shed was dark with rods of sunlight stabbing through the gaps between the logs. It smelled of machine oil and straw. She was fiddling with a long piece of binder twine, showing it to me, wrapping it and unwrapping it around a nail in the wall.

It was the piece of twine Mean Hughie had used to save her life.

We could hear the pigeons gulping up on the beams.

I said I wanted to kiss her and would it be all right.

Her eyes were green in a rod of sunlight.

And they were open wide, and they were full of water and she said yes, it would be all right.

Cast of Characters

Young Tommy	the hero
Baby Bridget	his friend with her poor arm
Dad	the hero's father, Tommy, a good singer and talker
Mean Hughie	a mean and troubled man
Aunt Dottie	the cleanest aunt a hero ever had
Frank	Dad's friend, one of the worst drivers in Canada
Poor Bridget	Baby Bridget's mom
Hector Aubrey	a huge butcher
Romanuk	owner of a store that sells everything
A turnip	what you could roll in the space where your heart was
Baz	a helpful truck driver
A bunch of Hendricks	a redheaded family
King	a gas station owner who gives you gin
A dam man	a man with a very scary job
Buck O'Connor	a man who lost a part of his ear
Irene	the girl in Frank's favourite song
Father Farrell	a waving priest

Crazy Mickey	the hero's great-grandfather from Ireland
Great Grandma Minnie	his wife for so many, many years
Old Tommy	the hero's grandfather, the farmer
Leona	older sister to Monica, Martina, Ursula, Lena
Monica	second sister to etc.
Martina	third sister
Ursula	fourth sister
Lena	youngest sister to Leona, Monica, Martina and Ursula
Gerald	older brother to Vincent, Joseph, Sarsfield and Armstrong
Vincent	second brother to etc.
Joseph	third brother
Sarsfield	fourth brother
Armstrong	kid brother to Gerald, Vincent, Joseph and Sarsfield
Father Sullivan	a determined and practical priest
The Hummer	a flood victim
Mr. Dragonfly	a love bug

and others, all, by the way, made up